Liza Lou

and the Yeller Belly Swamp

by Mercer Mayer

Aladdin Paperbacks

25 Years of Magical Reading

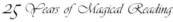

ALADDIN PAPERBACKS
EST. 1972

First Aladdin Paperbacks edition May 1997
Copyright © 1976 by Mercer Mayer

Aladdin Paperbacks
An imprint of Simon & Schuster
Children's Publishing Division
1230 Avenue of the Americas
New York, NY 10020

10 9

The Library of Congress has cataloged the hardcover edition as follows:
Mayer, Mercer.
Liza Lou and the Yeller Belly Swamp.
Reprint of the edition published by Parents' Magazine Press, New York.
Summary: With her quick thinking, Liza Lou manages to outwit all the haunts, gobblygooks, witches, and devils in the Yeller Belly Swamp.
1. Monsters—Fiction. I. Title.
PZ7.M462Li   1980   [E]   80-16605
ISBN 0-02-765220-3

ISBN 0-689-81505-0 (Aladdin pbk.)
(ISBN-13: 978-0-689-81505-8)

To my mother

One fine day, Liza Lou's mother said, "Apple Dumpling, I want you to take this tote bag full of sweet potatoes over to Gramma's house and cook them up for her. She's feeling a mite poorly.

"But mind you be especially careful when you cross the Yeller Belly Swamp."

"I will, Momma," said Liza Lou as she set off along the old swamp road. She'd heard tell about a good-for-nothing swamp haunt thereabouts who snatched away small children. And no sooner did she come to an old abandoned shed than she heard a terrible moaning and howling.

Sure enough, out of a broken window jumped a pale, nasty swamp haunt. "Liza Lou," that swamp haunt moaned, "I'm gonna snatch you away."

"Oh, Mr. Swamp Haunt," cried Liza Lou, "snatch *me* away if you must, but please, oh please, don't snatch away my tote bag full of sweet potatoes."

Now a swamp haunt may be good at snatchin', but he's none too good at catchin' on. Lickety-split, he snatched that tote bag right out of Liza Lou's hand.

"Oh, no!" cried Liza Lou. "Whatever you do, don't carry those sweet potatoes over to my Gramma's house, and please, oh please, don't cook them up in a pan." But before you could say—

"Yeller belly cottonmouth,
Possum up a tree,
You can catch the swamp fever
But you can't catch me"

that good-for-nothing haunt ran
clear through the swamp to
Gramma's house just so's he
could cook up those sweet
potatoes and make
Liza Lou miserable.

Now Gramma loved fresh-cooked sweet potatoes,
but she surely didn't like any good-for-nothing swamp
haunt messing around her kitchen. So, before she sat
down to eat—one, two, three—she picked up the
still-hot frying pan and shooed him right out the door.

By that time, Liza Lou was safe at home having
a fine sweet potato dinner with her mother.

The very next morning Liza Lou's mother said, "Sugar Plum, I want you to pole across the swamp and take these hot huckleberry muffins to your Auntie Jane. But mind you hurry over, because there's no sense dilly-dallying in that Yeller Belly Swamp."

Liza Lou did as she was told. No dillying under a bobcat, no dallying by a cottonmouth, and not a bit of dilly-dallying alongside an alligator. By and by, she came to Auntie Jane's.

After a tasty lunch of blackeye peas—with huckleberry muffins for dessert—it was time to pole back home.

"Liza Lou," said Auntie Jane, "if you will take this soiled Sunday-go-to-meeting finery, and boil it up, and scrub it all real clean for me by next Friday, I'll bake you a pecan pie of your very own.

"But get on home real quick now, so as you won't be out in that Yeller Belly Swamp after dark."

Liza Lou didn't have to be told twice. She knew all about the wicked swamp witch lurking out there in the reeds. If ever she caught you, there was no telling what she'd do.

Well, no sooner had Liza Lou poled 'round a big clump of cattails than a gnarled hand reached out and grabbed her. "Liza Lou," that swamp witch cackled, "I'm gonna boil you in a big pot of water, and then I'm gonna chew on your bones."

"Oh, Miss Swamp Witch," cried Liza Lou, "boil *me* in your big pot of water if you must, and chew on my bones as much as you like. But please, oh please, don't boil this precious little child I've got cradled in my arms."

Now everybody knows that a swamp witch is meaner than a stomped-on polecat, but not everybody knows that she is blinder than a cave bat.

Quicker than a blink, that old witch grabbed up the bundle of Sunday-go-to-meeting finery and pitched it into the boiling water. She snickered as she stirred and stirred.

But just because a swamp witch can't see worth a toot doesn't mean she can't sniff out a lie. "I don't smell no little child a-cooking in this pot," she said suspiciously.

"Why, Miss Swamp Witch," said Liza Lou, sweet as syrup, "then maybe you should smell a little closer." So the witch leaned way over the pot, and she sniffed and she sniffed.

"There ain't no little child in this pot at all," growled the witch. But before you could say—

"One, two, three, four,
Five on the double.
If you mess around me,
It's a mess of trouble"

Liza Lou pushed that old swamp witch—SPLAT!—into the pot of boiling water.

With a hoot and a holler the witch leapt right back out again and skedaddled into the swamp, a-screeching with all her might.

After a while, the Sunday-go-to-meeting finery was boiled all nice and clean, so Liza Lou fished it out and went on home.

When Friday came, her Auntie Jane baked her a pecan pie of her very own, which Liza Lou shared with her mother.

"Honey Child," Liza Lou's mother said one sparkly afternoon, "take this wagonload of junk and pitch it in the dump. But mind you watch your P's and Q's down by the Yeller Belly Swamp bridge."

Now Liza Lou took good advice when she got it, because she'd been warned about the slithery gobblygook living under the old swamp bridge. If ever he heard anyone crossing, up he slithered and gobbled that person for his dinner.

No sooner had Liza Lou crossed the rickety old bridge than, sure enough, the gobblygook crept up out of the mucky goo and said, "My, my, here comes dinner!"

"Why, whatever can you mean by that, Mr. Gobblygook?" said Liza Lou, bold as brass.

"That means I'm gonna gobble you up, right here and now!"

"Oh, that does make me feel better!" said Liza Lou. "Gobble *me* up if you must—go right ahead—but please, oh please, don't gobble up this valuable treasure I'm trucking in my wagon."

Well, a gobblygook, he doesn't know what a treasure is from what it isn't. He just likes to gobble. So he asked greedily, "Is that treasure any good for gobblin'?"

"Nobody gobbles treasure," said Liza Lou. "Everyone saves it."

"Child," said the gobblygook, "don't you tell me what to do, 'cause I gobbles anything I likes. And the first thing I'm gonna gobble up is that treasure."

And he commenced to gobble the whole wagonload of junk.

When he was done, he turned to Liza Lou. "Now I'm gonna gobble up you!" But try as he might, he couldn't even stand. He had gobbled far too much junk. That rickety old swamp bridge began to creak and sway. And before you could say

"Catch a turtle, catch a snake,
Catch a little froggy.
If you throw corn bread down the well,
It's going to get real soggy"

the slithery gobblygook sank—GLUB! GLUB!—
back into the mucky goo where he belonged.

"Well," thought Liza Lou as she drove her mother's empty wagon back home, "that bridge never was too safe anyway."

Bright and early the very next day, Liza Lou's mother said, "Hush Puppy, I want you to take this jug of blackstrap molasses over to the Parson's wife so's she and the Parson can have some with their breakfast hotcakes. But mind you be most particular when you pass the old well at the far side of the Yeller Belly Swamp."

"I will, Momma," said Liza Lou, because she knew all about the sly swamp devil who lived at the bottom of the well. If ever he caught anyone passing by, he jumped down inside his ear and stole his soul away.

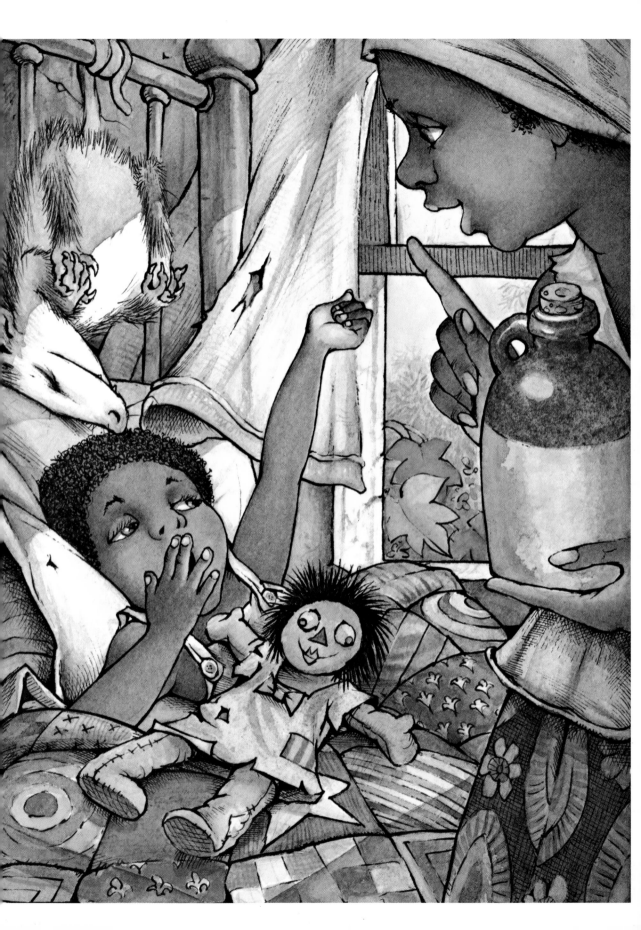

When Liza Lou got to the old well, there sat that swamp devil just waiting for her. "Liza Lou," he said, "I'm gonna jump down inside your ear and steal your soul away."

Now a swamp devil is mighty tricky, so Liza Lou knew she'd better do some pretty fancy thinking.

"Oh, Mr. Devil," she said, "I sure am glad to hear that! I thought you might steal away the soul I'm keeping safe inside this jug."

"Now what would I want with just any old soul?" that devil grinned. "It's yours I want, Liza Lou."

"Thank goodness," sighed Liza Lou, "because it's the Parson's soul I've got inside my jug. And it would be just awful if ever you stole that."

Of course, there's nothing in this whole wide world a
sly swamp devil likes more than a Parson's soul.

"Open up that jug, child," he wheedled, "and you just let
me see the Parson's soul." Well, Liza Lou let him take a peek.
"I don't see nothin' down there 'cept molasses," sneered the
swamp devil.

"I'm glad enough of that," said Liza Lou. "I was afraid
you might jump down inside to get a better look."

"Why, that's exactly what I'm gonna do!" said the swamp devil. And before you could say

> *"Cats are sneaky*
> *And a fox is sly,*
> *But the devil's best friend*
> *Is a bluebottle fly"*

that swamp devil turned himself into a fly and buzzed right down into the jug.

"There ain't nothin' down here at all!" hollered up the devil.

"Oh yes there is, Mr. Swamp Devil," said Liza Lou. "You are!" And with that she pushed the cork into the jug real tight.

Then Liza Lou delivered the jug just as her mother had told her. And the Parson and his wife sat right down to enjoy a nice breakfast of hotcakes and blackstrap molasses.

The Parson's wife poured some over her hotcakes. "Why," she said, "there's a fly stuck in this molasses."

"Well, my sweet," said the Parson, "why don't you just swat it?" And that's exactly what she did.

As for Liza Lou, she skipped all the way back home to her mother. And from that day to this, no one has ever seen hide nor hair of devils, gobblygooks, witches or haunts in the Yeller Belly Swamp. And no one misses them either.